For Charli

Penny Loves

PNK

Cori Doerrfeld

L B

LITTLE, BROWN AND COMPANY
New York • Boston

My name is Penny, and I love PINK!

I love my pink shirts . . .

. . . my pink shoes . . .

. . . and my sparkly pink sunglasses.

I love my pink parties . . .

. . . and I love my
pink potty, too.

I love pink cotton candy . . .

. . . pink ice cream . . .

. . . and riding my pink bike
past pink flowers.

I love everything pink!

I think I'd even love a pink monster!

Penny! Come meet your new baby brother!"

I don't like blue. I only love . . .

. . . pink!

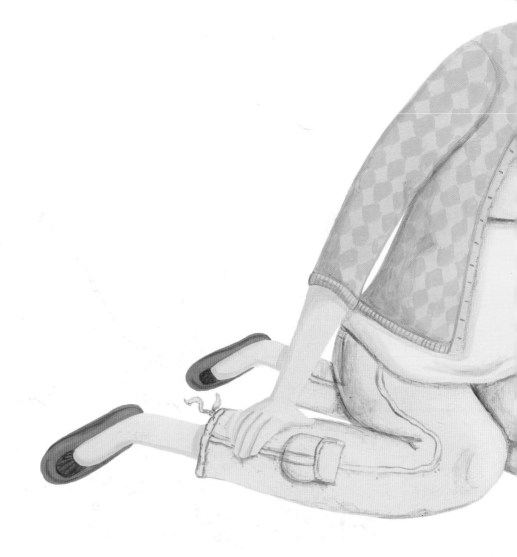

And I love YOU, Parker!